THE MOONPATH AND OTHER STORIES

Robert E. Swindells

Illustrated by Kathy Wyatt

Wheaton
A Division of Pergamon Press

A. Wheaton & Company Limited
A Division of Pergamon Press
Hennock Road, Exeter EX2 8RP

Pergamon Press Ltd
Headington Hill Hall, Oxford OX3 0BW

Pergamon Press Inc.
Maxwell House, Fairview Park, Elmsford, New York 10523

Pergamon of Canada Ltd
75 The East Mall, Toronto, Ontario M8Z 2L9

Pergamon Press (Australia) Pty Ltd
P.O. Box 544, Potts Point, N.S.W. 2011

Pergamon Press GmbH
6242 Kronberg/Taunus, Pferdstrasse I, Frankfurt-am-Main,
Federal Republic of Germany

First published 1979

Printed in Great Britain by A. Wheaton & Co. Ltd, Exeter (BW)
ISBN 0 08 022903 4

THE MOONPATH AND OTHER STORIES

For Vera Jacques

CONTENTS

THE MOONPATH

If the world were flat, and if you could look straight into the rising sun, you would see the land where Nick and Bruin lived. It was a land of sticky days and breathless nights, where the sun came up like an enemy and the wind had flies in it.

At the edge of this land, where bitter waves met hot sand, there lay a town of flat, ugly buildings and narrow streets and in one of these streets stood a blacksmith's forge.

Nick was apprenticed to the blacksmith. All day in his stiff leather apron he worked by the stinging-hot furnace; pumping the bellows or carrying bars of iron for his master. At night he lay on the dusty floor with a chain on his foot. Nick's mother and father had sold him to the blacksmith for seven years. Nick cried for them sometimes, in the night, but he hated them too, and vowed they would never see him again.

Sometimes Nick's master loaded the things he had made on to a handcart, and Nick pulled it through the town to the customers' homes. As he went along, Nick would search the faces of the people he passed. He always hoped for a smile, or a kindly word, but he never found one. It was a mean, ugly town full of mean, ugly people.

One afternoon as he was hauling the cart across town he saw that a small crowd had gathered in the square. There were shouts, and some laughter. Nick left the cart and went over to look. He was small and thin, and easily slipped through to the front. In the middle of the crowd, on a small patch of beaten dust, stood a bear. There was a collar round its neck with a

chain. A man held the chain in one hand and a stick in the other. As Nick watched, the man poked the bear with the stick and cried, "Down, Bruin!" The bear's legs collapsed and it rolled over in the dust and lay still, playing dead. The people laughed. Somebody dropped a coin in the man's hat. "Up, Bruin!" cried the man, and he jerked on the chain. The bear clambered slowly to its feet. Nick wondered what it felt like to have a coat of thick fur on such a day as this.

The man jabbed his stick into the bear's side. "Dance, Bruin!" he snarled.

The bear lifted its forepaws and began a slow shuffle on its hind feet, swinging its great head from side to side.

"Faster!" cried the man, and he struck the creature across its paws.

The people laughed. Bruin tried to move a little faster. There was a cloud of flies round its head; they settled near its eyes.

The man put down the stick and produced a battered mouth-organ. He sucked and blew a scratchy tune, and a few more coins fell into the hat. Bruin moved heavily to the thin music. After a while the man stopped playing and the bear dropped on to all four feet. People clapped a little. The man bowed and grinned.

Nick was turning sadly away when the bear raised its head and looked at him. The boy paused, gazing back into those tiny, pain-filled eyes. In that instant, Nick felt something that made his own eyes brim, and caused him to clamp his teeth into his bottom lip. He turned and began to push his way through the crowd. He felt the bear's eyes following him and could scarcely see through the tears in his own. He lifted the handles of his cart and went on without looking back.

That night, lying on the dusty floor with the chain on his foot, Nick thought about Bruin. He saw the fly-tortured eyes and the dry, lolling tongue and he murmured softly into the dark, "Some day, Bruin, we will leave this place, you and I. We will sail away to a land that is white and cold as the moon. There will be no flies there, and no chains." He moved a little and his chain made a clinking sound. He sighed, and closed his eyes. "One day," he murmured, and then he slept, while the cold white moon slid silent down the sky.

The next morning his master said, "Take this boat-hook to Caspar, the fisherman. You will find him on the sand, mending his nets."

When he stepped out of the forge the sun hit him and he screwed up his eyes. "This land is an anvil," he told himself. "The sun is a great hammer, and it will beat me on the anvil until I am bent and blackened like the end of this boat-hook." He wiped the sweat from his forehead and turned towards the sea.

Caspar was sitting cross-legged in the sand, mending a net. He looked up, squinting into the sun. "Ah, my new boat-hook is ready, yes? Give it here."

Nick handed it to him and stood wiggling his toes in the hot sand.

The fisherman examined the boat-hook and said, "Tell your master I am satisfied and will pay him tomorrow."

Nick bobbed his head, and was turning away when the man said, "I saw you, yesterday. Watching the bear."

Nick turned. Pale blue eyes regarding him, a twinkle in them somewhere. He nodded. "Yes. We are both slaves, the bear and I."

He knew he ought not to have said it. Suppose the man told

his master? His eyes, fearful, met Caspar's. The twinkle remained. "Have no fear," said the fisherman, softly. "I have no master, but if I had, it would have been the moonpath for me, long ago."

Nick did not understand. "The—moonpath?" he whispered.

Caspar nodded.

"What is the moonpath?" asked Nick. Perhaps this man was mocking him.

The fisherman raised his eyebrows. "The moonpath? Why, the moonpath is the road to freedom; a silver track that lies upon the sea."

Nick turned, to see warm, brown water moving slug-like in the sun. His lip twisted up. "I see no silver track," he said.

Caspar grinned, shaking his head. "It is not there now, little slave," he said. His face became grave and he patted the sand beside him. "Come, sit here and I will tell you."

Nick approached the man, half-fearful, and sat down. Caspar set aside his net, drew up his knees under his chin, and wrapped his thick arms around them. He gazed out over the sea.

"It is big, the sea," he said. "It is the biggest thing on earth, and the fiercest. To cross it you need a good boat." He glanced sidelong at Nick. "Slaves do not have boats. But sometimes at night, in the full of the moon, there is a way for them if they believe and are brave."

Nick waited. After a moment, Caspar nodded towards the sea. "Out there," he said, "When the moon is full, there is a path across the sea. It is long and straight, and at the far end lies a land as cool as this land is hot." He turned earnest eyes to Nick. "He who takes the silver path must travel quickly, for it melts with the dawn and is no more until the moon is full again."

The boy felt a lump in his throat and he gazed at Caspar through tear-filled eyes. "I have seen such a path," he choked. "It is made from light. No one can walk upon it. You mock me."

Caspar shrugged. "I told you. A man must believe, and be brave." He took up a net and began to work upon it as though Nick were no longer there.

After a while the boy blinked away his tears, got up, and walked towards the town.

Many days passed. One evening, at the end of a very hard day, Nick's master beat him and left him waterless. Nick lay, a long time crying in the dust. When he had cried all his tears, he sat up and rubbed his eyes with the heels of his hands so that the dust from them made a grey paste on his cheeks.

"I will not stay here," he told himself, "to be beaten and starved and roasted. I will run away. I will go tonight." And he crawled across the floor to where his master had left a large file. His chain was barely long enough, but by lying at full stretch he was able to get his finger-tips to it. He laid the blade across a link and, working rapidly, began to saw at the iron.

An hour he worked, then rested, gasping. He blinked away the sweat and went on. At midnight the link parted. Nick scrambled to his feet and stood, listening. The moon-washed streets were silent.

He left the forge on tiptoe, flitting from shadow to shadow along the road. He did not know where he would go. The town was surrounded on three sides by the desert, and on the other by the sea. The desert, then. He must try to cross the desert. He turned up an alley, and cried out in terror. His master came swiftly, crouching, the great hammer drawn back over a brawny shoulder. Nick whirled and fled.

"Runaway!" roared his master behind him.

His voice echoed all across the midnight town. A door was flung open. Then another. Lights moved in windows. People spilled out of houses. Nick swerved and ran on. The people were shouting to one another. His way was blocked. He spun round. Men, strung out across the street behind him, and his master like some squat ape coming with the hammer. He ran left. A figure crouched, spreading huge arms. He spun. There! A clear run. He gasped, pelting along the unguarded alley, and as he ran he cried out, without knowing it, the name of the only other slave he knew. "Bruin! Bruin! Bruin! . . ."

Breaking clear of the buildings he glanced over his shoulder. His master followed, closer now, his hammer raised high. Nick ran on desperately then stopped, skidding in damp sand. The sea! They had driven him to the sea! He turned, sobbing, and angled along the beach, dodging between huge rocks and leaping over small ones. He could hear the pounding of his master's boots and the rasping of his breath. He threw back his head and ran wild-eyed, mouth agape. He never saw the rock. It struck

him below the knees and he went headlong in the sand. He roll
and screamed, flinging up his arms to cover his face. His master
raised the great hammer. A cry. The hammer fell, kicking up sand by Nick's head, and then his master reeled, clutching his side.

A shaggy form swayed erect against the moon, snarling. Bruin! The bear turned, a short length of chain swinging at its neck. Nick gazed up at the great head and then beyond, to where the moon hung cool and full in the velvet sky. Cool and full. Caspar! The boy looked seaward, and it was there. "I believe!" sobbed Nick.

Men were coming, running quiet in the sand. He scrambled to his feet. "Come, Bruin!" he cried.

The sand sloped gently down, and they ran; not into surf, but on to rippled silver, cool and hard. "I believe!" cried Nick, and they moved out across the midnight sea.

And all along the shore the people stood, their mouths open, staring. One stuck out his foot and snatched it back, drenched with moon-white spray. So they stood, all night, gazing out to sea. From time to time someone would shake his head, or mutter something under his breath. And when it was near to dawn, they looked at one another out of the corners of their eyes, and shuffled their feet, and began to drift away in ones and twos. They walked by the blacksmith, who nursed his side by a rock. And the blacksmith said to one, "Where is my boy?", and to another, "What happened?" But they just shook their heads like people in a dream.

And then the bear's master came dangling the broken lock from Bruin's cage. Far, far away, a cooling wind ruffled Nick's hair and Bruin dropped his head to lap the snow.

RAJAH

The burning plain holds many dangers, and in the friendly jungle there are thorns; a cub has much to learn. There is a story that teaches some of these things. It is about a tiger called Rajah.

Rajah was born on the plain, at daybreak, and the gold of the new sun got into his coat. His brother was born that day, too, and his two sisters, but none of them was as big or as strong as Rajah. His mama licked him, purring. He would grow to be a prince, this one; like his papa.

Rajah's mama was wise. When she could, she lay still, and when she had to move she moved through bars of sun and shadow, where the gold and shadow pattern of her coat made her difficult to see.

When she was hungry, she killed. She killed the chital, which is swift, or the gaur with its deadly horns. And though nearby grazed the helpless goat and the stupid cow, Mama never hunted them, for the goat and the cow are the creatures of man. And when, as sometimes happened, a man came near the cover where she lay, Mama would rise quietly and slip away. Man has no claws. He is slow, and carries no horns on his head. Nevertheless, he is best left alone. All these things, and many more, she taught the growing cubs.

Little Rajah, though, did not always listen. Sometimes, while the others lay nuzzling their mama, Rajah would stalk an insect in the grass. He would move stealthily as he had seen his mama move. And when he was very close he would spring, snarling;

pinning the creature beneath a clumsy pad. He would toy with his prey awhile, then eat it, while the others sucked Mama's warm milk.

One day at sunset, when Mama returned from hunting, she stood a little way off and called the cubs to her side. Always before, she had left them to lie in a safe place until dawn, when she would come back heavy with meat to lie up and doze through the heat of the day. Now she turned with a low growl and led them on to the darkening plain.

The others went timidly, staying close to Mama; mewing now and then when startled by some shadow. But Rajah went boldly, swatting grass-heads with his paw. Once he even bounded out ahead of Mama and she growled a sharp warning. When he slunk back she cuffed a squeal out of him.

The kill was a chital deer. Mama made them lie still while she circled it, watchful; testing the air. When she was satisfied she called her cubs and began tearing at the rump. The little ones wrinkled their noses at the smell of meat. Mama dropped a strip of hide for them and they circled it, sniffing. Rajah moved in close, dabbed out a paw and licked the blood from his pad. Then he crouched, snarled and sprang. He wrestled a moment with the strip, then pinned it down and attacked with needle teeth, growling.

The others watched as their brother ripped the hide into bloody fragments and bolted them. They were hungry, too, but it was Mama's milk they longed for.

At dawn they left the remains of the kill and Mama led them into cover. Only Rajah and herself had fed. She lay down under a rock and allowed the cubs to suckle. Rajah, contemptuous, lay a little way off with his back to them, and growled a warning at the rising sun.

The months slipped by and the cubs grew. Soon they were accompanying Mama when she hunted. They watched as she pulled down the hefty gaur; seizing it by the throat and forcing its head down to the ground, twisting at the same time to make the creature topple. They saw how by caution she avoided the gaur's wicked horns: circling, awaiting her chance to dart in and seize.

Later, when they had grown almost as big as Mama, she would

maim a chital, then watch their clumsy efforts to finish it off. At first, they always failed, and Mama would step in at last to finish off their unlucky victim so that the family might feed. But little by little the cubs grew in skill and in strength until, when he was thirteen months old, Rajah pulled down a gaur without Mama's help and crouched with his teeth in its throat till it was dead.

From that night on, Rajah began to sever the ties that bound him to the family. In the daytime he would lie up with them in a shady thicket or rocky overhang, but at dusk he would rise, stretch and yawn, hard muscle rippling under his magnificent coat, and slip off alone. Sometimes he would return to lead Mama and the others to his kill. Sometimes, if the kill were small, he fed alone. He was losing patience with these cubs who were so slow to learn. Why could they not be more like himself? When he moved in the forest, monkeys shrieked their warnings and every grazing beast would cease feeding and move off. When they saw him coming, the jackals would scatter whining into cover. Sometimes it seemed to him that the very shadows on the forest floor shrank back at his approach, to make a path of sunlight for his feet.

And Mama. He was growing tired of Mama and her endless teachings. Could she not see that he was bigger than her now, and stronger? Did she not notice how all things stepped aside for him?

Mama, for her part, remained patient. He showed her how all things feared him and she said, "Yes, my son." He said that he was the strongest beast on the plain except for the elephant, and the elephant did not count because he was stupid and allowed man to capture him. And Mama said, "Yes, my son." He told her that, since all things were afraid of him, no creature existed that could harm him. And when he told her this, Mama said, sadly, "You are wrong, my son."

And so Rajah left her. He slipped away at twilight, and she never saw him again.

There now began a golden time for Rajah. He hunted well, fed well and every day grew more strong. The boundaries of his territory were wide, and if another tiger dared encroach upon it, he was driven off with wounds he would nurse a long time.

While his fellow males feared and hated him, he was beloved of every tigress on the plain. He moved like a sultan among them, contemptuous of their adoration, and he fathered many cubs.

When Rajah went forth there came always a great stillness. The forest seemed to cower like a thief in his domain, and the very plain held its breath. And Rajah went slowly; smooth as oily water; waves of muscle rippling his coat. His great head swung all the while from side to side. Arrogance smouldered in his yellow eyes and there was a contemptuous twist to his snarl.

One day, moving silently along a ravine, he rounded a bend and came upon some men. At the sight of him they fled, gibbering one to another in their fear. And Rajah stood, fully in sunlight, and watched their flight. "Beware of man," his mama had said. "Leave his path clear, and give him no cause to know that you are there." The men had been leading a goat and had abandoned it. Now it stood irresolute, a puny thing trailing a halter. Rajah lunged, and in an instant the goat lay dead, its neck broken. He opened its belly but did not feed; leaving it broken among the stones as a mark of his contempt.

When hunger drove him forth again at dusk, he went on up the ravine and stood in the fringe of trees, gazing down into the village. Cooking-fires burned here and there, and villagers came and went by their light. The wind carried a smell of cattle to his flared nostrils. Rajah settled himself in the scrub to wait.

One by one, the fires died until the village lay in darkness. Rajah waited. Now and then the sounds of voices reached him and dim lights flickered in doorways. When all was quiet, he rose and picked his way noiselessly down the slope and out across the compound of beaten earth. Passing like a shadow in the spaces between huts, he approached the shed in which the cattle were tethered. No need to stalk his prey this night. He entered the shed as though it were his own and the beasts lowed fearfully, jerking at their halters. Rajah selected his victim, seized it by the throat and toppled it into the straw. The stricken cow kicked for a moment and was still.

Smelling death, the other cattle rolled their eyes and milled in confusion, their cries filling the night. Men awoke, groping for clothing in the dim huts. But when they ran with their lamps and their guns to the cattle-shed they found only a snapped halter and a twist of bloody straw.

Rajah dragged his kill into the ravine and fed. The meat was sweet and the way he had won it much to his liking. And when he heard his mama's words inside his head he drowned them with a snarl.

When the village woke at dawn a herdsman found Rajah's pugmarks in the dust. A small crowd gathered and they squatted; tracing with their fingers the outlines of his pads; exclaiming over their size.

That night, Rajah entered the village again, killing and carrying off another cow. And though the hapless cattle made as much noise as before, no man left his bed. For the village people were poor. Possessing few weapons, they had learned to accept the ravages of tiger and leopard in the same way that they accepted famine, plague and drought.

Time passed. Rajah extended his range to take in a number of the villages that dotted the plain. Hunting, with its uncertainties, became a thing of the past for him. A tethered victim cannot flee and Rajah killed at will; knowing the fear his coming inspired, and revelling in it. "I am Rajah," he said. "All things fear me, and even man cowers in his den when I pass by."

Even man. His mama had been wrong. Man was weak. He had no claws, and his teeth were the teeth of a calf.

One day at dusk, Rajah came upon a porcupine in his path.

"Never dispute the right of way with a porcupine," his mama had said. "Rather walk round him, small as he is." But Rajah stepped aside for no creature. He flicked out a paw to swat the impudent beast, and leapt back snarling, a quill protruding from his pad.

He lowered himself on to his side and began gnawing at the quill. Presently it broke off level with the skin and he could bite it no more. He pulled himself erect, standing on three pads. When he tried his weight on the stricken paw the pain shot from pad to shoulder and he reeled with nausea.

Hungry as he was, Rajah could not hunt that night. He limped into a ravine and lay up, licking his paw.

The wound became infected. Rajah's pad swelled. It was agony to stand on, and he could not unsheath the claws. Hunger carved a lean arch into his belly.

In the third dusk after his encounter with the porcupine it drove him forth to hunt. He made for the nearest village, standing in the jungle-fringe on three pads. All was still. He left the trees and moved jerkily towards the cattle-shed. The scent of meat brought the saliva to his jaws and an ache to his belly.

He entered the shed, selected his victim and attacked. The tethered bullock jerked and bucked, lowing shrilly. It swung its head. He could not reach its throat. He shifted to try from a fresh angle, but the beast turned towards him, head lowered. He was not fast enough.

In desperation he came from behind; the tether preventing the creature from facing him. He reared, raking its rump, but with one sound paw he could not bring it down. Outside, men were calling to one another; running with their lamps towards the shed.

Rajah abandoned his victim and fled; bounding clumsily across the compound and into the sheltering trees.

He lay up nearby. Day came. The sun beat down. His head ached and his infected paw throbbed intolerably. And the hunger. Rajah had never known such hunger. It fed on his strength, sucking it into his belly where it melted like river mist.

He must eat. If he did not, he would soon be too weak to go forth; he would die cowering in his shelter like a . . . like a man.

He remembered the torches and the shouting, and his lip

curled in a silent snarl. He had fled. He, Rajah, whom every creature feared. Yet man was puny. He had neither claws nor teeth and he went slowly on two thin legs like a wingless crane. Man was helpless. Man was easy meat.

In the full glare of day Rajah went forth. Near the village he came upon women washing clothes in the river. He watched. Presently one of the women called something to her companions, gathered up her bundle and began climbing the bank.

Rajah crouched. The woman drew near, singing softly to herself. She topped the rise, passing from the sight of her friends. Rajah sprang. At his snarl she whirled, screamed once, and died. Rajah clamped his jaws in the thin body and dragged it into scrub. The other women fled screaming.

Easy meat. He fed, and lay content. The next day he went to the same place and took another woman. After that no women came to the river. Rajah switched his attention to a nearby village, killing a man as he worked in the field.

One day, as he limped up a dry ravine, the quill in his pad worked itself free. The swelling began to subside and within a few days Rajah was virtually whole again. He might have turned once more to the gaur and the chital for his food. He might easily have continued taking his toll of man's cattle. He might have, but he did not. The flesh of man was sweet and soft, and easy in the taking.

Terror now haunted the villages that lay within his territory. No man dared venture forth. Clothes remained unwashed and fields grew weedy with neglect. Rajah basked in the fear his presence caused. He killed, and killed again. If he could find no man on the plain, he entered a village, tore out the roof-thatch of a house and snatched his victim from the midst of a shrieking family. He had only to roar, and all life shrank from the sound. "I am Rajah," said the roar. "Stand in *my* path and you will die!"

Lying one day near the dirt road that crossed the plain, Rajah heard an unfamiliar sound. He raised his head, ears pricked. The sound swelled. Something moved in a cloud of dust upon the road, coming nearer. Rajah snarled softly as the vehicle passed, and wrinkled his nose at the acrid smell it left behind.

At twilight he rose and made his way unhurriedly towards the village. Moving silently up the shadowy ravine he stopped, nostrils flared. The night had the smell of cattle in it. Somewhere nearby a cow lowed uneasily. He rounded a bend, silently, and saw the cow. It stood in the dry bed, facing him, its halter twisted round a stump.

Rajah curled his lip in a contemptuous snarl. Man was even more stupid than he had supposed. Now he had taken to tethering his cattle in the open, where any creature that wanted to might pull them down. And more than that: this cow stood directly in Rajah's path. He crouched, muscles bunched. Nothing stands in Rajah's path, and lives. With a roar he launched himself at the terrified beast.

A cry, above him and to the left. Light stabbed into his face, searing his eyes. He swerved towards the dark. Another beam slashed along his flank, found his eyes and steadied. Pinned blind between the beams he froze and at once a volley of detonations ripped the night. Rajah leapt, screaming into the air and crashed down, his torn body threshing in white, blinding light. Another volley. The great body jerked convulsively, sagged, and was still.

And man, who has no claws; man the slow, whose teeth are the teeth of a calf, climbed down from his platform in the tree.

Rajah lies in man's bungalow now, on the floor, where the cubs of man can pull his ears and poke their clawless fingers in his snarl.

THE MERMAID

Karl Fischer was the second most eminent marine biologist in Soldavia, and he was jealous. After Zoltan Waldo he was the leading authority in the field.

After Zoltan Waldo.

For Zoltan Waldo had caught the extinct fish and now lived in a fancy apartment; and came and sat at Karl's table in the café and asked, in a sneering manner, how the little slides were going.

The little slides were Karl's bread and butter. He mounted specimens on them and sold them to the Education Ministry. At the café he ate soup, with sometimes a little bread, while Zoltan Waldo chewed steaks and beamed at him like someone's fat uncle.

Sometimes, when he could not face it any more, Karl stayed away from the café and heated himself some beans in the shack on the beach he called his laboratory, and it was on one of these occasions that the idea came to him.

He was scooping beans into his mouth and idly turning the pages of a magazine when his eyes came to rest on a drawing of a mermaid. He stopped chewing.

A mermaid. He dropped the iron spoon into the pan. An extinct fish is one thing. A mermaid is quite another.

For a long time Karl sat gazing at the drawing, while the beans in the pan cooled and congealed round the forgotten spoon. A mermaid.

Presently he rose from his chair, grabbed his coat and left the laboratory at a brisk walk.

There was in the Soldavian coastal town where Karl Fischer lived a street lined with run-down, unvisited shops; the sort of street which one is apt to find in small towns the world over. The painted signs were faded almost to nothing, and the shops along one side seemed to peer short-sightedly through their dusty windows at the shops along the other side. It was to this street that Karl's small, rapid footsteps carried him.

About half-way down on the left was a shop with a stuffed otter in the window. The otter had been there so long its coat was gingery yellow instead of chestnut brown and in its glassy eyes was a wistful look, as though it dreamt of rivers long since dry.

Jan Kapok, ancient, thin and balding, awoke on his stool with a start, and blinked at Karl over the top of his wire-framed glasses. His pale arms still lay folded on the counter where they had supported his head, until the tinkle of the rusty bell had disturbed him. Recognition dawned, and he rose stiffly to his feet, holding out a trembling hand.

"Karl! I am happy to see you, my friend. It has been a long time."

Karl nodded, taking the hand briefly. "A long time. How is business?"

The old man grunted, shrugged. "There is no business, Karl. A long time now, there is no business. I have a little put by, you know, and if it were not for that . . ."

"I know," Karl interrupted, one palm raised. "I know how things must be with you, and that is why I am here."

"What do you mean?"

Karl smiled. "How would you like to earn some money, old friend, eh?"

Kapok grunted again. "I would like that fine, Karl. There is no call now for taxidermy. It is a dying art, like thatching."

"I have work for you, Jan." Karl glanced all around, as if to assure himself that they were alone, then continued in a softer voice. "I need a friend I can trust."

Kapok leered toothlessly. "You can trust me, Karl," he said. "You know that. What is this—work? A fine fox, perhaps, with diamonds in his belly? Some little packets of white powder to help pad out a pike?" He shook, cackling. "I have seen it all before, y'know. Many times before."

Karl shook his head, half-angry. "No. It is nothing like that."

"Then what?"

"I want you to make me a mermaid."

"A—mermaid?"

Karl nodded. "A fake, but a thing of quality. I am not going to put it into a fairground sideshow."

The old man lowered himself on to his stool. "What then *do* you propose to do with it?"

"I shall allow it to make me famous," smiled Karl. "And rich, of course. Think of it." He ran his fingers along the headlines of imaginary newspapers. "SCIENTIST CAPTURES MERMAID. SOLDAVIAN PROVES EXISTENCE OF MYTHICAL BEAST." He dropped his hands and laughed, exultant. "That will bring down the high and mighty Zoltan Waldo a peg or two!" He slapped the old man's thin shoulder, almost knocking him to the floor. "We shall see *then* who eats all the steaks, eh?"

Kapok clung shakily to his perch. "This is all very well, Karl," he protested. "But it is not simple, this thing. It is not like fifty years ago. There are tests today—X-rays, that sort of thing."

Karl laid an arm across Kapok's shoulders. "You can do it, Jan," he said. "You, the finest taxidermist in all Soldavia. For you it is a small thing, my friend."

Flattery prevailed, and after a moment Kapok nodded. "Very well, Karl. I will try. But . . ."—he looked at Karl sternly over his glasses— ". . . it will take time. You must allow me time, or your plan will never succeed."

And so it was that a few minutes later Karl emerged from the dingy shop and walked back to his laboratory, whistling all the way.

Within minutes of Karl Fischer's departure, Kapok began work. From the ancient deep-freeze in his backroom he took the corpse of a female orang-utan. This he placed in a long glass tank containing brine. Then he put on his coat, hung up a yellowing sign with "Closed" on it and locked up the shop.

He went down to the fish-dock, where he spent some time

haggling with a man who finally sold him a fine marlin, undertaking to deliver it to the shop that same evening.

His next call was at the workshop of a man who stuffed mattresses. Here he bought a quantity of long, pale hair which, the proprietor assured him, was human. With this, and certain other small purchases, Kapok returned to the shop.

That night, when the rest of the street was shuttered and still, a lamp burned weakly in Kapok's back room. The body of the ape lay on a marble slab and Kapok crouched over it, a tray of surgical instruments at his side.

He opened the animal to expose the tube that had carried air from mouth to lungs. At its lower end the tube divided into two, one section feeding each lung. He removed the tube and, with meticulous care, sealed off the holes which this left in the lungs. A fish has no lungs, but it has swimming-bladders; sacs filled with air which help it to float. He felt confident that anyone examining the creature now would take the sealed lungs for swimming-bladders.

He sat back and stretched, yawning. Now the mermaid must be provided with a means of breathing underwater. It must have gills. The marlin had a fine set of gills and he would work on that tomorrow. He got up, turned down the lamp, and went to bed.

The next day he removed the marlin's gill apparatus and implanted it in the ape's head, just under the ears. It was a precision job and he was exhausted when it was over. The mermaid now had swimming-bladders and gills. It had legs which it ought not to possess, and it lacked a tail.

The following day, Kapok took a scale from the marlin and put it under a microscope. The rings on the scale told him how old the marlin had been. He jotted down the figure and went to look at the teeth of the ape. Luck was with him. Both creatures had lived about four years. It would not have done to have had a four-year-old mermaid with a twenty-year-old tail! He grunted his satisfaction and went off to a café he knew of where you could sit all day over a glass of wine and a dish of peanuts.

Refreshed, he went to work early the next morning. He cut both creatures in two and fastened the trunk of the ape on to the marlin's tail. He did it with great skill; joining up the two

INS-AND-OUTS
ORANG-UTANS
BRONCHIAL
CONGESTION
GLUE
CANNULAE

spinal columns and making the digestive tract continuous. It was evening by the time he had finished. He placed the mermaid in the brine-tank and gazed at it in the lamplight. "You're a little ugly, my dear," he sighed. "And we shall have to do something about that."

He spent many days making the mermaid beautiful. He did something to the flat, wide nose, so that it became tip-tilted and rather fine. He gave her long, pale hair that fell golden about her shoulders. He altered the eyes until they flashed impishly at him under long, curled lashes. He gave her fair skin and pearly teeth and when she was finished he sat for an hour, just looking. "If only I could breathe life into you," he whispered. Presently he sighed, rose from his stool and went off to fetch Karl Fischer.

By ten the next morning, the shack laboratory was thronged with newsmen and Fischer was holding a press conference. Behind him, in a tank, floated the mermaid.

"It was a routine trip," said Karl. "Down the coast, trawling for specimens. I do it all the time." He leaned forward, palms flat on his desk-top. "Only this time it was different. This time when I hauled in my net. . . ." He turned, indicating the mermaid with a sweep of his hand. "Gentlemen. You see before you incontestable proof of the existence of a creature which for centuries has been regarded as mythical."

He paused, to let the significance of his words sink in. The newsmen gaped at the mermaid, turning slowly in its tank. One of them raised a hand. "Sir," he said. "Was it . . . she . . . was the mermaid dead when you first saw it?"

Fischer nodded gravely. "I fear so." He lowered himself into his chair, rested his elbows on the desk and made a steeple of his fingers. "You see," he continued. "It is my opinion that these creatures live at a considerable depth, and far from any coast. That is why they have so seldom been seen. This one," and again he waved a hand towards the mermaid. "This one must have become lost, and strayed too close to the shore. She was entangled in my net and when I hauled it aboard the sudden change of pressure must have killed her. "He gazed, wistfully, into space. "Poor creature. As I bent over her, her eyelids fluttered their last, and a tiny bubble appeared at the corner of her mouth. But there. . . ." He shrugged, and sighed heavily, while a brave smile hovered on his lips. "That is science, gentlemen. She holds out a prize, only to snatch it away."

The reporters nodded, scribbled on their pads, and left.

Some people came with a van, and the mermaid was carried away to the Department of Natural History at the university. Here it was subjected to rigorous examination and pronounced genuine.

Karl Fischer's name flashed around the world and when, on one occasion, he appeared on television with Zoltan Waldo somebody was heard to ask, "Who's that with Karl Fischer?" A few months later he accepted, with becoming modesty, a science prize which made him wealthy.

He took to appearing again at the café where once he had eaten soup. "I will have the venison," he would say. "A haunch, with truffles. And to follow I will have a salad of tropical fruits, specially flown in, and drowned in cream, sugar and brandy. And carry it past Waldo's table." Life was very sweet.

Then Zoltan Waldo disappeared. He came no more to the café, and the phone in his apartment rang unanswered. For six months it was as though he had vanished from the face of the Earth. When he reappeared, he had a mermaid just like Fischer's, and an abject Jan Kapok in tow.

Waldo hauled his mermaid up to the university, threw it on a slab, and proceeded to demonstrate to an audience of stunned academics exactly what Fischer's mermaid was made of.

For Karl there remained only ruin, disgrace and humiliation. Stripped of his prize, he was tried for fraud, found guilty, and sentenced for life to the penal colony on Kopi-kopi, an island in the tropics consisting almost entirely of guano: there to work with the other convicts, digging out the filthy stuff and trundling it by the barrowload to the dock, under a pitiless sun.

There was a guard on Kopi-kopi named Janosh. He was fat, with droopy black mustachios, and he glistened in the sun. Every time Karl passed with his barrow, Janosh would grin. "Seen any mermaids today, Professor?" he would call, and laugh; throwing back his head and slapping his knees.

One day, Karl was working alone near the beach; jabbing his shovel into a towering guano-bank, lifting, and tipping the stuff into an iron barrow.

White heat warped the land and shimmered on the sea, and as Karl paused to wipe the sweat from his brow he heard someone singing. He rested his shovel and gazed all around, for nobody sings on Kopi-kopi. He looked, but there was only the bank, and Janosh standing on top of it, against the sky, with his hands on his hips.

He turned. The sea was a heaving mirror that shot sun-flashes at him, but there was a cluster of rocks, too, and on one of them. . . .

He dropped the shovel and wandered down to the water's edge like a man in a dream; head thrust forward; screwing up his eyes. The mermaid wriggled an iridescent rump and looked at him over her shoulder. She was fixing something in her hair.

He held out his hands, mouth agape. He wanted to speak; to ask something of her, but he was paralysed. A camera. Oh, if only for one sweet instant he had a camera. Or a witness. The next best thing, a witness. Janosh. He turned, feet in the sea. The guard was a warped blob on the glare. He tried to yell but all that came out was a croak.

And then she laughed and he spun to face her; for some reason suddenly conscious of the stubble on his cheeks. Her head was thrown back, and she was laughing. He swallowed, twisted his neck round and yelled, and when he looked again she was gone.

He filled the barrow, mechanically, and pushed it up the bank. Janosh stood, hands on hips, grinning. "So what's with all that yelling?" he demanded, as Karl drew level. "What's all the noise for, eh? You seen a mermaid or something, maybe?" And he threw back his head, and laughed.

THREE LITTLE KITTENS

He lifted the box out of the boot, placed it on the verge and straightened, glancing both ways along the road. There was no other traffic. He slammed down the lid and walked quickly round to the offside. There he paused, his hand on the door-handle, before striding back round the car to push the box on to its side with his foot. A moment later, the driver at the wheel, the car slid forward, U-turned and roared off towards the city.

Tai-lu pushed a flap aside and emerged on to coarse, mud-spattered grass. She was a white-pawed tabby, her eyes just turning green.

Pinwheel followed, gazing a moment after the dwindling car.

Mew remained curled in a corner of the box. A shiver rippled her coat, for she felt the cold without the snug proximity of her sisters.

Tai-lu and Pinwheel explored, though neither strayed far from the box. They had been born in the box and therefore it was home. It was to the box that Mother would presently return, to feed and to clean them.

A pale sun sank beyond autumn trees. The shadow of the hedge stretched across the verge to touch the road. Pinwheel shivered, returned to the box and settled herself beside Mew. Their mother had not returned and she was hungry.

Tai-lu crouched beneath the hedge, listening. Something had moved nearby, rustling the dry leaf-carpet on which she stood. She turned her head and saw a vole. It was sitting on its hind legs, cleaning its whiskers with fussy fore-paws. Its black eyes stared straight at the kitten. Tai-lu sprang. It was an inept, kittenish move and when she skidded to a halt in a shower of leaves the vole was gone. Tai-lu sniffed among the gnarled stems, perplexed, then fell to licking the dust from her coat. Presently she left the hedge-bottom and began picking her way over the verge towards the box. Mother was the hunter. Mother would bring them food.

Twilight dimmed into night and a thin wind sang in the hedge. Tai-lu circled the box, calling, but there was only the voice of the wind. After a while she went in, moulded herself into the bony curve of Pinwheel's back, and slept.

Dawn. The verge was lightly touched with rime and fields of silver grey receded into mist beyond the hedge. Tai-lu stirred, disturbing Pinwheel, who stretched. Mew flinched, shivered and called plaintively in half-sleep; one eye a sticky slit. Hunger invaded their small bodies; drove sleep away and settled in: a cold, sullen ache.

Tai-lu uncurled, got up, and padded stiffly to the wet rim of the box. The sharpness of the dawn pricked her nose so that she sneezed. Gingerly placing a pad in the crisp grass, like a bather testing the sea, she emerged, innocent, into that first motherless day.

The others followed her out. Pinwheel sniffed among the wet grass-roots, then chased her tail; a game she played often, and which had earned her her name. Mew's eye was still closed and she moved in on Tai-lu; nuzzling her sister's flank and calling for their mother.

A lorry roared by. Its acrid exhaust awakened in Pinwheel an echo of yesterday, and she ceased her whirling and stood, watching the vehicle until a bend in the road took it away from her.

Tai-lu moved away towards the hedge. She had remembered the vole and her hunger burned. Mew trailed after her but Pinwheel remained, gazing along the road. Tai-lu called her, sharply; the mother-call. Pinwheel turned her head and, seeing only her sister, hesitated. Tai-lu repeated the call and Pinwheel began to follow, slowly.

The hedge-bottom lay rich in scent-tracks, but nothing moved among the crisping leaves. The kittens fanned out, following their noses. Tai-lu's track meandered along the hedge, then led out across the stubble-field beyond. She followed, but lost it at a place of torn earth and stiff white roots.

Pinwheel stalked a finch that fed on haws, but a leaf cracked under her pad and the bird was gone.

Mew, tracing the path of a shrew, found its hole among the stems and stood, calling piteously.

Tai-lu, out among the stubble, also called and they followed her; through short, hard stalks and frosted chaff to a wire fence and beyond, where long brown grass gave way to crowding trees. On they went, down dim, vaulted aisles between the beeches. Frost had failed to penetrate here and they trod paths of wet brown leaves like coins on the ground. Scents tantalised them of creatures who had been there before; their paths forming an invisible lattice across the forest floor. Yet they saw no living thing except the birds that flitted through the tree-tops.

Presently the wood thinned, and Tai-lu found herself at the top of a grassy, shallow slope, at the foot of which lay the buildings of a farm.

She stopped. Sounds and smells reached her, half-familiar. Pinwheel came up and stopped beside her, tasting the air, while Mew came trailing through the trees, calling continually.

A door opened, and a woman threw something from a plate into the yard. She remained a moment framed in the doorway, then went in, leaving the door open. A smell of cooking drifted up the slope.

Pinwheel started forward. Tai-lu stood, one fore-paw raised, and called. Pinwheel hesitated without looking back, then went on down the slope, picking her way between tussocks. Tai-lu watched her sister a moment, then turned her head to look at Mew. Her gait was unsteady and the ailing eye remained closed. Tai-lu went back to her and began to clean her coat.

Pinwheel came to the farmyard gate and stopped, gazing across the muddy yard. The smells of people and of cooking, and the sound of human voices washed over her so that she tingled. Inside her head she saw a picture of her mother, wise and warm by the flickering fire. She squeezed between the slats and trotted out across the friendly yard.

She was bolting the first bacon-scrap when the dog came round

the side of the house. He was a Border collie, lean from herding sheep, and any scraps in *this* yard were his. He stood for an instant, teeth bared, then hurled himself snarling towards the starving kitten.

Pinwheel whirled and fled, but the dog, schooled in the ways of herding, threw himself between his quarry and the gate. Pinwheel swerved towards the house, but the woman blocked the doorway, shouting. Pinwheel streaked away along the house-front and out, making for the wall. The dog was closing in and she leapt, scrambling to the top, and threw herself out and down and away up the slope.

The dog cleared the wall and came bounding in pursuit. Pinwheel zigzagged up the hill, tiring. The dog was gaining on her. A few seconds more, a final lunge and his jaws would close across her back. And then there was Tai-lu, running beside her and then swerving away, making for the trees. The dog checked for an instant, chose Tai-lu, and bounded after her.

Pinwheel hurled herself with the last of her strength into a sapling thicket and cowered, panting in the copper leaves.

Tai-lu ran swiftly, chose her ground and turned, a trunk at her back and twisting roots to either side. The dog closed in. Tai-lu arched her back and struck, spitting. Needle-claws raked his muzzle and the dog leapt back yelping. He pawed the wound, shook his head and lunged in again. Tai-lu stood her ground and lashed out. The collie backed off snarling, a bright bead of blood on his mouth.

Tai-lu spat defiance at him and after a moment he turned, trotting away with his tongue lolling and his tail down.

They left the vicinity of the farm, though Pinwheel dragged a little and looked back wistfully in spite of her clash with the dog. Humans to her meant warmth and food, and mother. She longed to be near them with a longing as fierce as her hunger. Nevertheless, when Tai-lu called, she followed.

Deep in the dim wood they flushed a blackbird, fat with summer, which trailed a wing and fled from them with short, lopsided hops. Tai-lu bounded in pursuit. The crippled bird, blind with panic, began to circle. Tai-lu ran arrow-straight, gained rapidly and rolled him screeching into the leaf-mould. He fought desperately and twice broke free, to flutter erratically across the ground; till Pinwheel leapt in to add her weight and they pinned him, this pair of spitting furies, and he died.

They fed, ravenously. Mew, half-blind and weakening, was jostled by her sisters and ate little, and when they moved on, leaving two curled feet and a drift of feathers, she began to fall farther and farther behind.

Tai-lu did not travel far, however. No longer hungry, she became aware of her tiredness and, coming upon a fallen tree, she squeezed into a dry hollow under its roots. Pinwheel joined her, followed after a while by Mew. They huddled together for warmth, and slept.

Pinwheel woke first, and raised her head. A sleety rain fell hissing through the trees. It was colder, and something was wrong. She shifted, uneasily. Inside the curve of her belly, Tai-lu responded with a twitch. Mew, curled along her back, did not stir.

Pinwheel got to her feet. Mew toppled forward into the space she had left, and lay still. Pinwheel nuzzled her, and called. Tai-lu raised her head, rolled over, and came to her feet. They licked their sister, and nuzzled her, and called to her many times, but she slept on.

And so they left her there, in a dry, dark place where hunger could not reach. They padded away through the rain, and Tai-lu stopped from time to time to look back. But though she looked very hard, and waited a long time, no little form came calling through the trees. And so after a time she stopped looking.

Towards evening they left the wood and emerged upon a narrow road. They followed its downhill meander, travelling in the verge where a grey scum of sleet lay among the grass-roots. Now and then a vehicle passed and the kittens crouched till it was gone.

As it grew dark the verge-dwellers emerged and went about their nightly business. Presently a vole darted from under Pinwheel's pads and the sisters gave chase. Pinwheel flushed it from the verge and as it ran out upon the road Tai-lu rolled it over, pinned it and killed it with a nip of her teeth. Tai-lu carried the vole into the hedge-bottom and they ate, noisily. Afterwards they cleaned themselves and curled up under a hawthorn root to sleep.

The cold dawn roused them and they moved on, stiffly, and presently the road led them by the first scattered buildings of a village. Tai-lu went warily, slipping silently from shadow to shadow, but Pinwheel went boldly and wistfully; rubbing her draggled flank on the corners of houses; savouring doorsteps with their rows of empty bottles.

They were almost through the village, Tai-lu pressing onwards, when a door opened and a child stepped out on to the path which bisected a neat cottage garden. Pinwheel stopped to peer at the child through the white-painted fence, and was seen. The child cried out. Tai-lu, at the corner of the fence, called sharply. Pinwheel glanced towards her sister, but remained looking through the fence. The child ran indoors and returned carrying a dish which she placed on the path, at the same time making coaxing noises and extending a fluttering hand towards the kitten.

Tai-lu called again, urgently, and the eyes she turned on Pinwheel said, "Come away, sister. Come away with me now, before it is too late." And Pinwheel gazed back, and her weak, affectionate features said, "I am sorry, strong one. If I could, I would be like you, but I cannot. I need them, with their rugs and their food and their firesides." She turned from Tai-lu and passed easily through the slats of the fence.

Tai-lu watched as her sister crouched between the knees of the squatting child, lowered her head to the bowl, and submitted to the hand's caress. She remained outside the fence, watching and hoping. But when the bowl was empty and the child carried it indoors Pinwheel followed, and was gone.

And so now she was alone. Tai-lu the strong, the independent. Tai-lu the free.

Yet she lingered in and about the village; stealing at dead of night up to the sides of houses to snatch from rubbish-bins that which she would not take from human hands. She took her rest in sheds, and barns, and outhouses.

She teetered thus, half-wild, as autumn gave way to winter. She grew wild-eyed, lean and wise. Always there, yet seldom seen, she spurned man's fickle affections while living off his waste. Sometimes, ghosting in frosty silence by a locked and bolted door, she would feel warmth from the sleeping house and pause to let it fall upon her flank. Or lying at dusk in the draughty space beneath a shed, she would watch the light that spilled from glowing panes upon the snow.

And as winter deepened, Tai-lu's pride faltered and she took to hanging around doorways in the early mornings, until somebody took pity on her and brought out food. Only, when they crouched down with it, inviting her to approach, she hung back. Hung back against the urge to submit, and in spite of her aching hunger. So that presently her benefactor would throw down the food and retire. And from such hollow victories she derived her only comfort.

There is in most lives a moment at which their future course is decided: a moment when the last, vital factor falls on to the scale, tipping it. This moment came for Tai-lu on a grey, cold morning as she kept furtive watch on the shop across the street. It was early, and the butcher in his stained white apron had the street to himself as he trimmed his window. Tai-lu knew that presently he would open a side-door into the alley and dump a double armful of offal, scraps and bones in a bin there. She would wait until the first customer came, then cross over and oil her way up to the side of the shop to hook out scraps from under an ill-fitting lid.

As she watched, she became aware of something moving stealthily along house-fronts to one side of the shop. A shadow, moving in shadows; silent and intent. It drew nearer, until it stood in the spill of light from the butcher's window. She stiffened, teeth bared in a silent snarl.

The big tom stood motionless, fully in the light, and watched the open door. His frame was lean and his coat was long, and the wind that ruffled it bore the tang of the woods to her across the gleaming street. Tai-lu shivered. Some of the tenseness left her body, and she found herself swept by an unknown sensation beneath which her hunger ceased to ache.

Here was nobody's cat, and he gave off pride like light, and she knew by his very stance that he had not come for scraps.

He watched the door. Beyond it, the butcher went to and fro; hacking at something on his block, carrying the pieces to add to his display.

He bent in the window. The big tom moved; bounding over

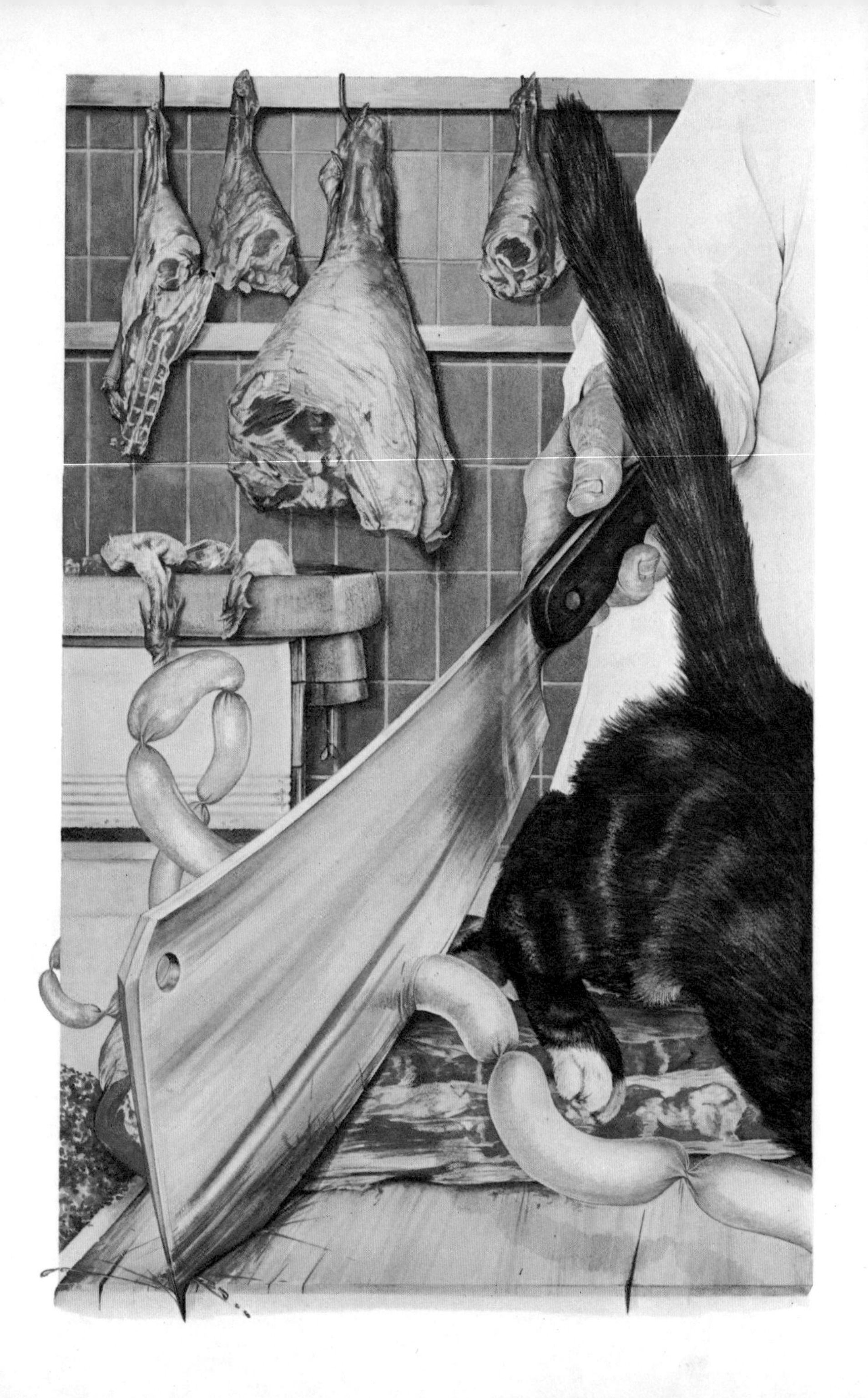

the single step, round the counter and up, to crouch on the gashed and bleeding block. The butcher turned, cried out and leapt, the cleaver bright in his upraised fist. The big tom, jaws clamped on meat, leapt aside as the blade came down. The butcher lashed out with his foot, jerked the cleaver free of the block and threw it. The bright steel skittered under the bounding cat and he dropped the meat, streaking for the door.

On the step he whirled in a tight arc, dashed between the butcher's boots, snatched the meat, vaulted the counter and leapt through the doorway.

Like an arrow he came across the street and into the alley where Tai-lu crouched. She drew back into the shadows. The big tom turned, dropped the meat and straddled it with his fore-paws. The butcher came to the edge of the pavement, glared into the alley and retreated, muttering.

The big tom sensed he was not alone and turned, gazing at Tai-lu with cold yellow eyes that said, "There, you cringing stray. When you can take without asking, then you will be free."

He ate facing her; tearing and bolting the meat he had won; coldly indifferent to her hunger. When only a scrap remained he rose, stretched and went stiff-legged to the mouth of the alley.

The wind drove sudden sleet along the kerb, and he turned into it as she crept forward to fall upon the scrap that he had left. He looked back, knowing she would be there, and the cold yellow eyes said, "This way, little one: yonder lies freedom, and its price. Into the wind, and never look back. I look back to you; I, who never look back. Let this be the measure of my regard and follow, if you will."

And Tai-lu stepped over the scrap, left the alley, and turned her face into the wind.

THE PLASTIC-EATERS

Lenny "Buck" Tooth eased up spacetramp's nose, hit the retros, and dumped his battered ship on the pad. Dust drifted against the green sky, settling. Lemmon detached himself from the cluster of buildings and came towards the ship.

Tooth operated the airlock, snapped off his harness and swung down from the cabin.

"Hi, Lemmon. How's pioneering?"

Lemmon shrugged, hands thrust deep in the pockets of faded dungarees.

"You know how it is on this glorified asteroid; just one durn thing after another. Got the chicken-wire I radioed for?"

Tooth nodded. "Yeah. It's in the back. That's not gonna keep out the dust-devils though."

Lemmon grimaced. "It ain't dust-devils I'm worried about. Got 'em licked with the wind-break." He nodded towards a line of new saplings. "Now it's them plastic-eaters."

"Huh?"

"Plastic-eaters. They don't have a name really; still unclassified 'cause we ain't reported 'em yet, but that's what we call 'em."

Tooth had opened up the cargo doors and was busy hauling out Lemmon's order; dumping packages of food, tools and clothing on the hand-truck. He paused, turning. "Plastic-eaters? Why d'you call 'em that?"

"Because they'll eat anything in reach, just so long as it's plastic."

Tooth laughed. "I don't believe it. It's one of them gags all you settler boys try to pull on us Earth-basers, ain't it?"

"No it ain't!" retorted Lemmon. "You drop that stuff a minute and come on over here, and I'll show you if it's a gag or not."

They left the pad and Lemmon led Tooth towards the clutch of low domes that constituted the farm buildings. He stopped by one of them, bent down, and lifted a ragged flap of the clear plastic wall material. "This stuff's supposed to be indestructible. Fireproof, stormproof, frost resistant and all that jazz. Look here." He moved a stubby thumb over the flap. "These here are teeth-marks. The whole panel's all chewed up." He straightened. "Every dome's the same; even the house."

Tooth laughed again. "Eaten out of house and home eh, Lemmon?"

"T'ain't so durn funny neither," snapped Lemmon. "I've lost tool handles, containers, boots and lotsa other things. Shelby over at New Acron lost a whole barn. I'm just hoping they don't eat chicken-wire too. Gonna fence in the whole damn farm. No other way."

Tooth shook his head slowly. "Funniest thing I ever heard," he said. "And I've hit every inhabited rock in the system."

They went towards the house. "If you ain't rushing off," offered Lemmon, "Deb and me'd be glad to have you stay the night. Be dark soon." He screwed his eyes into a sky that had become indigo.

Tooth grinned. "Thanks. I've got some stuff on for the Shelby place, but it'll do in the morning. How is Deb anyhow?"

"Fine. Little Earthsick I guess, now and then."

"Ain't we all?"

"Yeah." Lemmon looked at him sidelong. "Y'know, Buck," he drawled, "with all the angles you got in that brain of yours, I'd have thought you'd have gotten yourself a nice little number on Earth before this."

"Nope. T'ain't easy, Lemmon. Guy was telling me you'd need thirty thousand a year on Earth now just to get by. Plus a hundred thou or so to build a little house someplace in a non-pollution belt."

He stopped talking, abruptly, and a thoughtful expression

clouded his eyes. When they reached the house he greeted Deb in a perfunctory manner, and was quiet all through dinner.

Later, they sat on the porch and Lemmon said, "Penny for 'em, Buck."

"Huh?" Tooth grunted. "Oh, sorry, Lemmon. Sorry Deb." He pulled himself up in the chair. "Lousy company, I guess, and such a nice dinner too."

"What is it, Buck?" asked Lemmon. "Another of them angles?"

Tooth grinned. "Maybe so, Lemmon," he said. "Maybe so." He got up out of the chair. "If you folks'll excuse me, I reckon I'll sleep on it now. Tell you all about it at breakfast." And he shambled off, hands in pockets. Deb raised her eyebrows at Lemmon, and Lemmon shrugged. They locked up and went to bed.

At breakfast, Tooth could scarcely eat for excitement. "Lemmon boy," he said, "my days as a freight-jockey are over. I'm gonna have that little house I was talking about *and* a nice steady number back on Earth."

Lemmon poured coffee, looked at Tooth through the steam. "Sounds good, Buck," he said. "What's the angle?"

Tooth leaned forward, his eyes shining. "Plastic-eaters!" he cried. "Them cute little furry things you was telling me about. *That's* the angle."

Lemmon intercepted Deb's quizzical glance and his shrug was barely perceptible. "What d'you mean, Buck?" he queried. "What's plastic-eaters got to do with anything?"

Tooth waved a bit of toast at him. "Listen, friend. It's been a long time since you was on Earth. D'you know what the Earth is now?" He waited for no answer. "A dump, that's what it is. A great big lousy dump. And for why?" He snapped at the toast, chewed rapidly and swallowed. "Plastic, that's why. The whole goddam planet's buried in plastic. D'you know . . ."—his eyes shone with an almost manic light—". . . that with all of our technology and goddam know-how we still ain't come up with any way to dispose of plastic waste? They've filled up every damn hole on the planet with plastic bottles and cartons and bags, and now they're building mountains out of 'em." He threw out his arms in an eloquent gesture. "You can't take a walk on the beach without wadin' through plastic flotsam. Some of it's more than two hundred years old."

Light dawned in Lemmon's slow grey eyes. He laid his big hands on the table and rose out of his chair. "Buck boy, you're a genius!" he breathed. "Why all you have to do is . . ."

"Right!" Tooth pushed back his own chair. "All *you* have to to do is have a half-dozen of them varmints waiting for me next trip. Tell Shelby. Just six, that's all. Alive!" He paced the floor, slapping a fist into his palm. "I'll hire 'em out by the hour. Fifty bucks the hour. No, dammit, a hundred. They'll pay. I'll get rich *and* be the saviour of the goddam planet all at the same time." He began getting into his gear. "It's the perfect angle!" he cried. "It can't lose."

Something occurred to Lemmon. "Hey, Buck," he said slowly, reluctant to break in on Tooth's venal fantasy. Tooth, zipping up a boot, looked up.

"Yeah?"

"What's in it for me?" said the farmer. "Me and Shelby, I mean?"

"Oh!" Tooth came to his feet, grinning. "Oh, now don't you go frettin' yourself about *that*. D'you think I'd sit back there on Earth growin' richer by the minute and you out here scratchin' for vegetables in the dirt? No way, old buddy. Why, you and Deb'll be off this lousy rock quicker'n you can spit!"

Lemmon shook his head. "Can't get off, Buck. You know that. Twenty-year contract with the land-grant."

For an instant, Tooth looked nonplussed. Then his brow cleared. "Well then!" he laughed. "We'll just have to make this the most luxurious goddam farm in the galaxy! Can't you just see it?" He turned to the window with a sweep of his arm. "Out there we'll build a pool, so you can look right out the window at it. We'll have a patio, too, with lattice and vines, and somma that expensive furniture for loafin' around in. And while you're puttin' in lotsa loafin' time up here on the patio . . ."—he widened his gesture to take in the whole arid farm—". . . out there the robo-tractors'll be doin' your ploughin' and plantin' and liftin' and sich! Why . . ."—Tooth's eyes filled with tears for the sheer beauty of his invention—". . . you won't hardly know you ain't back home, Lemmon. You'll be rollin' in it, boy!"

Ten minutes later, Spacetramp lifted off and Lemmon went indoors to call Shelby.

When Tooth returned the following month, Lemmon presented him with six live plastic-eaters in a cage. Tooth gazed raptly at the rabbit-sized creatures through the mesh. "Ain't they beauties?" he breathed. "Ain't they just gorgeous?"

They sat together for the last time on Lemmon's porch, and talked of pools, and patios and robo-tractors until it was time to go to bed.

In the greenish dawn they shook hands and Tooth lifted off. Deb and Lemmon stood on the pad and waved till his tail-flame faded.

Tooth hit Earth in a record four days, shut himself in his apartment and wrote some letters. He wrote to senators and ministers, to kings and to captains of industry. In his letters were words like environment, conservation, pollution and godsend. The word dollars was mentioned too. He sat back to await the response.

It was not long in coming. Each morning saw a fresh pile of letters on Tooth's threadbare mat, bearing stamps from around the globe. He would scoop them up and sit hunched over the table, wielding a paper-knife and cackling to himself with glee.

Would he please bring his plastic-eaters to Atlanta, to Dallas, to London, to Newport, to Lagos? Would he come at any time convenient to himself, and would he accept payment in escudos, marks or yen?

At first he went by train, plane and copter-cab: hurrying from dump to dump across the face of the planet, dangling a wire cage in one hand and an overnight bag in the other. Then one day he stopped long enough to read his bank statement. He turned two shrieking somersaults on the worn carpet, picked up the phone and bought a jet. He hired a man to fly it, too.

His visits to the apartment became fewer, and when he did come home he could scarcely push open the door for the piles of mail behind it. He moved out, found a secretary and put her in an office.

So fond did he become of his penthouse apartment in the Presley Building that he grew reluctant to leave it, even to work. He put an ad. on TV, interviewed some applicants, and hired a man to do the travelling for him. Now he could really put in some sauna-and-sunroom time.

12.34

A year went by. The Earth's plastic mountains shrank while Tooth's bank balance went into orbit. The newspapers called him "Captain Cleanup" and "The Munch-Munch Millionaire". He had dinner at the White House, and the Friends of the Earth said he ought to be President.

Sometimes he talked to reporters. One of them said, "Sir, why don't you tell us where these plastic-eaters come from, so we can get more of 'em here on Earth?" And Tooth's sleek, bronzed body shook with laughter and he said, "Kill off the goose that lays the golden eggs? You think I'm crazy—or what?" And the reporter went away and wrote a piece about him, in which he hinted that maybe Buck Tooth wasn't quite such a goddam good guy after all.

One day he had a letter from Lemmon. "Dear Buck," it said. "We heard you was doing okay back there. Feller told me you was a millionaire already. How's about my pool, old buddy, or maybe a little of that fancy furniture? Your pal, Lemmon. PS. Shelby sends his best."

He filed it in the waste-paper basket.

A little girl wrote to him. She said the town where she lived was awful ugly, but it was such a small town she didn't suppose he'd ever visit it with his plastic-eaters. Did they ever have babies, and if they did, might she please have just one? She'd take real good care of it because her pet rabbit had just died, and his hutch was a comfy one with a bedroom upstairs and all.

Tooth dictated a reply to his secretary. It said:

Dear Lois,

My plastic-eaters are far too busy to have babies, and little girls like you ought to be busy in school instead of writing silly letters to busy grown-ups.

Lois's mother sent this reply to a newspaper, and the newspaper printed it. People began muttering against him, but he was too rich to care. They could not reach him. There were bodyguards at his door and his number was not in the book. He bought up the newspaper and sacked the editor who printed his letter.

Lemmon kept writing. Tooth showed an envelope to his secretary. "If we get any more like this," he said. "I don't even want to see 'em. Throw 'em right in the shredder."

Then they escaped. Nobody knew how it happened, but when Tooth's man went to pick up the cage one morning the door was open and the cage was empty.

He looked everywhere. He called Tooth. Tooth sacked him and called the police. The police brought in dogs. Nothing. Tooth put ads on TV. He put ads in the newspaper he had bought. He offered large rewards. Nothing. Tooth called his broker. "How much am I worth?" he asked, and when he had the answer he shrugged, smiling. "So it's over," he said to himself. "So what? Who needs more than thirteen million dollars anyhow?" He sacked his secretary and sat back to enjoy his wealth.

When the airliner crashed, nobody thought much about it at first. Airliners crash all the time. The experts poked around like they always do, looking for something to blame. Then they found some wires from the plane's electrical system. The plastic insulation sheath was missing. They found the body of a small animal, too.

The phone rang in Tooth's apartment. When he picked it up a voice said, "Sheaffer, *Daily Globe*. They found a plastic-eater in that plane. Any comment, Mister Tooth?"

"Yeah," said Tooth. "Nuts!" He hung up.

Next day another plane crashed, and a luxury liner was blacked out in mid-Atlantic. They found a dead plastic-eater in the plane, and two live ones on the ship.

Tooth's lawyer called. "They're suing you," he said. "They'll take you for millions."

Tooth blanched. "Millions?"

"Yessir, Mister Tooth. Millions."

Tooth hung up, and sat for a long time gazing without seeing at the wall of his beautiful room.

The plastic-eaters bred. Coming as they did from another planet, they had no natural enemies on Earth. The Earth was kinder, too, than their distant home. It was warmer, there was more water about, and everything on the planet seemed to contain large quantities of delicious plastic.

Planes were grounded, ships lay idle and cars refused to start. In Seattle, a tower block built in a revolutionary new material tilted, groaned and fell. Desperate governments put a bounty

on plastic-eaters. Every one killed was worth a dollar. Cities bristled with airguns, traps and baits. It made no difference.

Newspapers, when they appeared at all, carried headlines like "MUNCH-MUNCH MONSTER MUST MAKE AMENDS", or "RICH RECLUSE REFUSES RAP". One read simply: "EXTRACT TOOTH!"

They caught him on the Mexican border, trying to cross over with a canvas bag stuffed with banknotes, Krüger rands and diamonds. They arrested him. The charge was that of importing an unregistered alien species without a permit.

When they tried him the court-house was jammed. The judge was late because his car would not start, and one of the jury came barefoot because something had eaten all his shoes. It was a short trial. The jury scowled at him throughout and their foreman pronounced him guilty in a voice tinged with hysterical joy, before turning to acknowledge the applause of the spectators.

The judge called for order, and turned to gaze down upon Tooth. "It is the sentence of this court," he intoned, "that you be taken from this place to the State Penitentiary, and from there to one of the frontier planets, where you will remain in penal servitude for a term of twenty years."

Tooth rounded on his attorney. "Penal servitude?" he howled. "Frontier planets? There's no such penalty!"

The lawyer shrugged. "There is now," he said.

It took the prison ship a month to reach its destination. The airlocks slid open, and the convicts emerged, shielding their eyes from the greenish light. Shouting wardens jostled them into trucks, which would carry them to the farms where they would work. One by one the trucks growled into life and moved off.

Tooth sat glumly by the tail-gate of the bouncing truck, dreaming of pools and saunas and fat cigars, and wondering where in the goddam galaxy he was now. The truck stopped, and the tail-gate clattered down. A boot touched his ankle. "C'mon, Tooth," growled a warden. "Get on down. This is where you stay."

He rose, stiffly, and dropped on to the dusty track. Somebody slammed up the tail-gate and the truck rolled on down the road. He turned. A farmer stood silhouetted against the sun.

"Hello, Tooth," said Lemmon.

THE FELL-DOG

The wind boomed against the house, flinging rain at the window. David shivered, sitting on the wide sill. It was cold here by the window. But then it was cold all over Aunt Em's house. How did she stand it? How could she live here at all, on the edge of the soggy moor where it never seemed to stop raining?

He thought longingly of the warm, neat house his parents had in Leeds. A house in a row of houses where most of his friends lived, in an avenue that led down to the main road—to shops and coffee bars and the football ground.

He wished his mother had not gone into hospital. He wished his dad did not work away, then he could have stayed at home till Mum was better. Aunt Em was Mum's aunt really. She must be about a hundred and fifty years old.

He pressed his cheek to the rain-beaded pane, gazing across the sour garden where nothing grew. Beyond the iron gate lay a narrow road that wound away between the hills. Somewhere at the end of that road was a village. It might as well be on the moon.

"Three weeks," he muttered, turning from the window to survey the high-ceilinged, cheerless room in which he sat. "Three weeks and it's rained every single day." A coal fire flickered in the grate, flinching when the wind roared in the chimney.

He turned back to the window and his eyes were drawn to a movement, high up on the fellside. Sheep always grazed there;

dotted about the slope like boulders and, like boulders, apparently windproof and impervious to rain. Now they were running; bunched together and running down the slope, then across, then up. They paused, milling, then they were off again in a new direction. David screwed his eyes through a mile of flying rain, but he could see no cause for their panic. He shrugged, sliding off the sill, hands in pockets. They were always doing it. He had seen them a few times and it puzzled him. He left the room and wandered along the dim corridor to the kitchen, where his great aunt was doing the breakfast dishes.

"Shall I wipe them for you, Aunt Em?" he asked.

"Nay: there's nowt much to it," said the old lady. "It'll only take me a minute."

David leaned against the dresser. "You know the sheep," he said. "Up on the fell?"

"Aye." She did not turn round. "What about them?"

"Well, sometimes they just start running. They're standing there all peaceful and then they run, all together, as if something's after them, but there's nothing there."

Aunt Em slotted another dish into the rack. "It's just the way sheep are," she said. "Daft." There was an edge to her voice.

"They act scared," said David.

"Scared?" The old lady's tone became sharp. "What's to scare them up there, eh?" She turned, snatching up a tea-towel with soapy hands. "Take after your Uncle Sam, you do," she snapped. "He was always bothering himself with stuff like that. You'll leave well enough alone lad, if you've any sense."

David shrugged. "I'm not bothered really. It's just queer, that's all." His great aunt's reaction had startled him.

Aunt Em picked up a cup and wrapped the tea-towel round it. When she spoke again her voice was softer. "You're fed up, I expect, cooped up all day in this place and nobody to play with. Why don't you get wrapped up and go for a bit of a walk? The fresh air will do you good."

He didn't fancy it. The wind rattled the kitchen window. Still, it would make a change. He nodded.

"I think I will. Where's a good place to go?"

The old lady chuckled drily. "Nay: one way's as good as another around here." She thought a moment. "You could go up and look at the viaduct. It's the local wonder of the world. Took 'em eight years to build and another four to blast a tunnel through the fell at the end of it. Settle to Carlisle Railway."

David put on wellingtons and an anorak and let himself out. The wind tore at his hood and drove needles of rain into his face. He pulled the gate to and set off up the road, his head down.

Half a mile up, the road went under one soaring arch of the viaduct that spanned the valley. David stopped, gazing up into the booming curve of brickwork. Thousands of bricks—millions probably. Each one fitted in place by somebody's hand. He shivered, thinking about a rickety scaffold a hundred years ago in the wind, and men working on it.

He was about to walk through when a voice called, "Amazing, isn't it?" He spun round. A man leant against the brickwork, lighting a pipe. He smiled at David through the smoke, hunching his shoulders to shield the flame from the wind. David went over. "Didn't see you," he said. "You made me jump."

The man grinned ruefully. "Sorry. You from the village?"

David shook his head. "No." He jerked a thumb along the road. "I'm staying at the old house back there. Fellside, it's called. With my aunt."

"Ah!" The man obviously knew the house. He was silent for a moment and the smile in his grey eyes gave way to a thoughtful look. "The old lady: is she well?"

David nodded. "Oh yes. Are you a friend of hers?"

The man did not answer. Instead, the grin came back and he said, "You're from the city, aren't you?"

"Yes, Leeds. How d'you know?"

The man laughed. "What d'you think of life in the wilds?"

David shrugged. "A drag really. Nowt to do. I was asking my aunt about the sheep."

"Sheep?"

"Why they run."

"Ah! They run from the Fell-dog, young man."

"Fell-dog—what's that?"

The man took the pipe from between his teeth. His expression became grave. "The Fell-dog," he said, "is a phantom. A spectral hound that haunts the fell. It hunts to fill a belly that cannot be filled, and so its hunger will burn for ever."

David shivered. Then he grinned. "You're putting me on, aren't you?"

The man shook his head. "No, lad. Indeed I am not." He moved, walking from under the arch out into the open. David followed. The man pointed at the viaduct with his pipe-stem. "When they were putting this up," he said, "there were a number of unexplained happenings. Noises at night. Howling. Most of the workers were Irish. Some of them claimed they saw a dog, at night or in misty weather. A giant dog with slavering jaws. Others laughed at them. Irish imagination, they called it. Then a man went missing. It was misty. They found him on the fell. His throat was torn out. After that they didn't laugh much. Stayed close. Others vanished though, from time to time."

He clamped the pipe between his teeth and fished in his waistcoat pocket, pulling out a gold watch. "And now I must leave you." He tucked the watch away. "Nice talking to you." He stuck out a hand. David gripped it briefly. It was cold. "Now and then," the man said, "the farmers around here lose a few sheep. They blame it on dogs. They don't know how right they are." With that he turned and strode off, coatless, through the rain. David gazed after him. Then he shrugged, turned, and began to walk back towards his aunt's house.

He did not tell Aunt Em about the man at the viaduct. He said he had enjoyed his walk and was not so bored now. Not so bored! He could scarcely wait for the day to end. He would stay awake tonight. He would have his bedroom window open a bit and listen for the Fell-dog.

The hours dragged by. Lunch, and a grey afternoon during which the wind dropped and the rain slackened to a drizzle, falling through mist. Dinner at seven o'clock, then a long evening by the fire pretending to read; watching his aunt crochet.

At nine he said good-night and went up the creaking stairs to his room. He raised the sash window a little, undressed, and lay between the sheets in the dark, listening. The hiss of the rain was muffled by the mist. The grandfather clock downstairs chimed the quarters, sounding far away. His curtain moved a little in a draught. At ten his aunt climbed the staircase and shuffled past his door to her room. A floorboard creaked. Silence.

He must have dozed, because when it came it jolted him;

echoing through distant hills, receding. He lay rigid, his heart pounding. Had he been mistaken? Dreamt it perhaps? There was only silence now.

He slipped out of bed, crossed to the window and moved the curtain aside. The rank scent of wet earth seeped into the room. It was impossible to see anything through the mist. He was about to return to his bed when the night was torn by a howl that spoke of utter desolation. He recoiled, dropping the curtain. His every instinct shrieked at him to slam tight the window and take to his bed, and yet before he knew it he was groping for his clothes; tugging them on in the cold black room while the hills threw back the echo.

On the landing he paused, listening. No sound came from his aunt's room. He went down the stairs, wincing at every creak; pulled on his anorak in the hall.

He let himself out quietly and slipped into the mist. At the gate he looked back. The house was gone. He shivered. His shoes tapped briefly on tarmac, then he was climbing through coarse tussocks and sodden sphagnum. His own progress made the only sound. The mist enveloped everything. He was blind.

Somewhere up the slope he sensed movement, and froze. Something was coming down; something so heavy that he could feel the thudding of its progress in the ground. He glanced round, wildly. To his left, barely visible, lay a boulder. He side-stepped, crouched; merged with its dim bulk, unbreathing; screwing his eyes into the murk. Formless blobs came at him out of whiteness, drumming; swerved, hurtling by so close he saw flared nostrils, rolling eyes. In an instant they were gone; swallowed up, gouts of breath dissolving in the mist. And behind them came the reason for their flight.

Looming noiselessly like a stain on the milky silence it stood to test the wind. Its fetid odour drenched the night like evil. Cold as the rock he clung to, David watched the massive head that swung, nostrils wide to sniff the scent of fear. He saw eyes like yellow lamps, a lolling tongue. For moments it stood, foul plumes of breath about its gaping jaws. Somewhere something bleated, and it stiffened, eyes blazing down the slope. Then it leapt, bounding down, and as it went it trailed a ghastly howl.

For seconds David remained crouching, sick with horror. He

must move. Must fly to lights and walls and people. To the cheerless house of his aunt that now seemed so inviting. But his way lay down the fell, and in that direction the hound had gone.

He ran, crouching; senses stripped and raw, flinching from sound and scent. He fled stumbling down the haunted fell, and the drizzle plastered hair across his eyes and sphagnum sucked his feet. Then the ground flattened and he stumbled, sobbing, out upon the road. He crossed, and stopped. There was no wall here, no gate. He had hit the road too high, or too far down. But which? Which? His head swung left then right. The silence made a picture in his head: the hound, rigid, casting for his scent or for the tapping of his shoes along the road.

With stifled sobs he went up on to the verge, going left. A hundred paces up he kicked a stone. The click was drowned in howling and he knew that he was being hunted. He ran, heedless now of sound, along the wet tarmac. And somewhere on his left, across the road, a thing was keeping pace along the fell.

Something loomed. He recognised a corner of the garden wall and gibbered in relief. Twenty strides and he was through the gate. A swishing of wet grass and the click of claws on tarmac. Shrieking, he flung himself at the door, scrabbling for the latch. It clicked and swung inward, flinging him headlong into the hall. He rolled, lashed out with his feet at the door, slamming it in the face of the thing that had bounded up the path.

He could see the dawn behind the curtains in his room. His aunt was in the chair beside his bed. Her face was grey. "Tell me about the man," she said.

"Man?"

She nodded. "You have been asleep. You talked in your sleep about a man."

David's eyes darted to the window. "The dog!" he croaked. "Is the window closed? I saw the dog, it . . ."

The old lady laid a cool hand on his forehead. "I know about the dog," she said quietly. "The window is closed and we are quite safe. Tell me about the man."

"He was by the viaduct," whispered David, "smoking a pipe. He had no coat on. He asked about you. He had a gold watch."

Aunt Em held something close to his face. "Like this?" she whispered.

David gazed at the watch. "Yes," he murmured. "It was exactly . . ."

"And the man," she interrupted him, holding up a fading sepia photograph. "Is this him?" There was a break in her voice.

David nodded. "Who is he, Aunt Em?"

The old lady got up and busied herself with the bedclothes. She did not answer him, but spoke very softly, as though to herself. There were tears in her eyes. "Oh, Sam," she said. "Why did you go out that night? They told you to leave well enough alone. And why do you walk the road without your coat? Can't you sleep, my dear?" She dropped the photograph on the quilt and hurried from the room.

David picked up the photograph. Great Uncle Sam smiled out at him; the same smile he had worn yesterday, under the viaduct. Great Uncle Sam, who died thirty years ago, at midnight, on the fell.

David gazed at the watch. "Yes," he murmured. "It was exactly . . ."

"And the man," she interrupted him, holding up a fading sepia photograph. "Is this him?" There was a break in her voice.

David nodded. "Who is he, Aunt Em?"

The old lady got up and busied herself with the bedclothes. She did not answer him, but spoke very softly, as though to herself. There were tears in her eyes. "Oh, Sam," she said. "Why did you go out that night? They told you to leave well enough alone. And why do you walk the road without your coat? Can't you sleep, my dear?" She dropped the photograph on the quilt and hurried from the room.

David picked up the photograph. Great Uncle Sam smiled out at him; the same smile he had worn yesterday, under the viaduct. Great Uncle Sam, who died thirty years ago, at midnight, on the fell.